ZEYNEP

The Seagull of Galata Tower

Story and Pictures
Julia Townsend

Zeynep is the seagull of Galata Tower.

BLACK SEA

Rumeli Feneri

Riva

Anadolu Feneri

B O S P H O R U S

Anadolu Kavağı

Yalıköy

Beykoz

Incirköy

Paşabahçe

Çubuklu

Kanlıca

Fatih Sultan Mehmet Bridge

Anadolu Hisarı

Kandilli

Vaniköy

...ngelköy

...rbeyi

...Bridge

ASIAN
SIDE

THE ISTANBUL BOSPHORUS

The Broader View

AUSTRIA SLOVENIA HUNGARY MOLDOVA UKRAINE
CROATIA YUGOSLAVIA ROMANIA RUSSIA
BOSNIA AND HERZEGOVINA
ITALY Adriatic Sea ALBANIA MACEDONIA BULGARIA Black Sea GEORGIA
Tyrrhenian Sea Ionian Sea GREECE Aegean Sea Istanbul ARMENIA IRAN
Sea of Marmara TURKEY
Mediterranean Sea SYRIA IRAQ
CYPRUS LEBANON
LIBYA ISRAEL & PALESTINIAN TERRITORIES JORDAN SAUDI ARABIA

Bostancı

ZEYNEP

The Seagull of Galata Tower

Çitlembik Ltd.

First edition: 2003
Color Separation: NEF Grafik
Printing and binding: Berdan Matbaacılık

ISBN: 975-6663-32-4

Published by Çitlembik Publications
Şeyh Bender Sokak 18/4 Asmalımescit Tünel
80050 Istanbul TURKEY
Tel: +90212 252 31 63/292 30 32
Fax: +90 212 292 34 66
www.citlembik.com.tr
www.nettleberry.com

The tall Galata Tower rises in the center of Istanbul in the country of Turkey and overlooks the beautiful old city. Zeynep lives on the roof and keeps watch over the Bosphorus, the Marmara Sea, the Topkapi Palace, and the Golden Horn. She often glides on the sea breezes and makes circles around the Tower.

When tourists take pictures, Zeynep poses proudly for them. She is very proud of her position at Galata Tower—maybe too proud.

One day a young seagull came and rested on the balcony. After a moment, Zeynep said, "You cannot stay here. *I* am the seagull of Galata Tower."

"What does that mean?" asked the stranger.

"It means that I live here and watch over the Tower day and night… just like my father did, and my grandmother, and my great grandmother, and my great, great grandfather. My family came with the Genoese from Italy. We've been here since before the Sultan Mehmet conquered this city over 500 years ago! Who are you? How long has your family been in Istanbul?"

"My name is Fikret, but my family doesn't live here," the other seagull replied. "I just arrived from the Black Sea this morning and I am very tired. This tower looked like a good place to rest."

"Well, I'm afraid you can't rest here," said Zeynep coldly.
"No birds can sit on the Tower but me."

Fikret was too exhausted to argue, so he flew away.
Zeynep didn't think about him again.

Entrance

Sometimes Zeynep would stand near the entrance
to the Tower and watch tourists come and go.
Children also liked to play soccer there.

The children who played in front of the Tower weren't always nice to Zeynep. One day, some children who were playing there threw rocks at her!

Zeynep took off quickly. She flapped and flapped, but suddenly she felt a terrible pain in her wing where a rock had hit her. She couldn't go any higher, so she landed on a nearby rooftop.

She sat there all day. Her wing became stiff and it hurt when she tried to move it. "Tomorrow it will be better," she thought.

But the next day it wasn't any better and, what's more, Zeynep was hungry. "Help!" she called to a seagull flying by, "Help! Help!" But the other seagull didn't hear her.

"Help!" she called to some pigeons standing on the next roof.

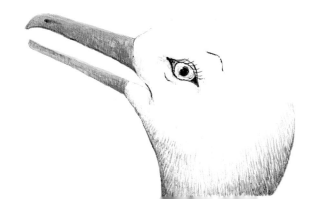

"Hmmf!" they answered. "Zeynep the Seagull of Galata Tower!
You never let us sit on your tower. Why should we help you?"
And they flew away.

Zeynep was alone. It began to rain. "Will somebody please help me?" she cried, but nobody was listening. She fell asleep as darkness fell. While she slept, she dreamt.

She dreamt that a seagull came and brought her a delicious fresh fish.

She dreamt that the seagull came again and brought her
more fish. Soon she could feel her wing getting better.

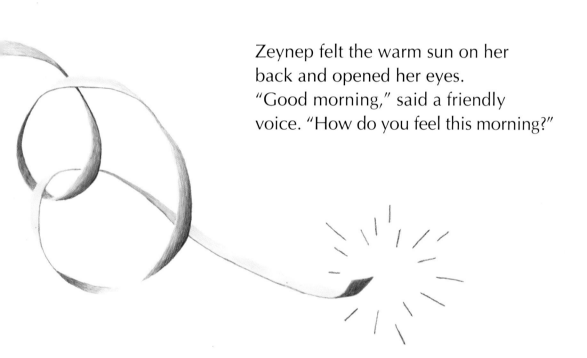

Zeynep felt the warm sun on her
back and opened her eyes.
"Good morning," said a friendly
voice. "How do you feel this morning?"

"Oh!" said Zeynep, with surprise.
Who did she see?

It was Fikret, the seagull from the Black Sea.

"I feel much better," she said, standing up and spreading her wings. "I dreamt that someone brought me fish to eat and that I could fly again."

"That wasn't a dream!" said Fikret. "By chance, I found you on this roof. You didn't look well, so I brought you the fish."

"How can I thank you?" cried Zeynep. "You helped me to fly again!"

"You can be my friend," answered Fikret. "I am new here in Istanbul and all on my own! I need a friend."

"I understand now that I need a friend, too," answered Zeynep.

Zeynep and Fikret spread their wings...

...and together flew to the top of Galata Tower.

And when the other birds saw them together
at the top of the Tower, they joined them.

And now Zeynep and all her friends watch over the Bosphorus,
the Marmara Sea, the Topkapi Palace and the Golden Horn
together. And Zeynep is ever so pleased to have her new friends!

THE GALATA TOWER

The Galata Tower, located in Turkey's largest city, Istanbul, was built in 1349 by the Genoese who at the time ruled over a semi-independent colony in the otherwise Byzantine controlled area. Derived from the Italian word "calata", which means "the road to the sea", the Tower of the appropriately named Galata area dominates its strategic location, commanding a view of the meeting of the waters of the Golden Horn, the Bosphorus Strait and the Sea of Marmara. At 61 meters (180 feet) high, obviously the crown jewel of the Genoese fortifications, it has had a colorful, albeit turbulent, history.

Only a century after its construction, the Tower was damaged during the Ottoman Mehmet's conquest of the then-Byzantine city of Constantinople, today's Istanbul. It was later repaired by the new rulers, only to suffer major damages once again during the earthquake of 1509. What's more, the entire Tower was burnt in 1794 and 1831 and again damaged in the storm of 1875, as well as another earthquake in 1894. After the rooms at the very top collapsed in 1959-1960, it was subsequently largely restored to its post-1831 state and reopened in 1967.

The Galata Tower has been used for various purposes throughout its long history. In Ottoman times it housed prisoners of war who were made to work in the shipyards. For many years it was used as a fire watchtower (hence the irony of its burning in 1794 and 1831). At one point the Tower served as a clock with midnight being sounded by drum rolls from its very top. A spectacular highlight in the Tower's history was when it became a springboard for Hezarfen Ahmed Chelebi, who in the 17th century donned man-made wings, leapt off the tower and "flew" to the opposite shores of the Horn.

Today equipped with an elevator that takes visitors up to its very summit in a matter of seconds, the Tower is frequented by locals and tourists alike who come to enjoy its breathtaking view as well as the restaurant, café and souvenir shops that it currently houses. For a modest fee you, too, can enjoy a visit to the home of Zeynep the Seagull, the Galata Tower, in the heart of the imperial city of Istanbul.